NIRVANA FOR GEN X

Abhirup Bhattacharya is a graduate in fashion technology from the National Institute of Fashion Technology (NIFT), Kolkata, and has completed his MBA in finance from Narsee Monjee Institute of Management Studies (NMIMS), Mumbai. He is also the author of *Winning like Virat: Think and Succeed like Kohli* (2017) and *Winning like Sourav: Think and Succeed like Ganguly* (2018).

Hailing from the City of Joy, Kolkata, he is presently based in Mumbai. He can be reached on Twitter @abhirupbh.

NIRVANA FOR GEN X

REDISCOVER YOUR INNER ZEN

ABHIRUP BHATTACHARYA

Published by
Rupa Publications India Pvt. Ltd 2019
7/16, Ansari Road, Daryaganj
New Delhi 110002

Sales centres:
Allahabad Bengaluru Chennai
Hyderabad Jaipur Kathmandu
Kolkata Mumbai

Copyright © Abhirup Bhattacharya 2019

The views and opinions expressed in this book are the author's own and the facts are as reported by him which have been verified to the extent possible, and the publishers are not in any way liable for the same.

All rights reserved.
No part of this publication may be reproduced, transmitted, or stored in a retrieval system, in any form or by any means, electronic, mechanical, photocopying, recording or otherwise, without the prior permission of the publisher.

ISBN: 978-93-5333-625-7

First impression 2019

10 9 8 7 6 5 4 3 2 1

The moral right of the author has been asserted.

Printed at HT Media Ltd, Gr. Noida

This book is sold subject to the condition that it shall not, by way of trade or otherwise, be lent, resold, hired out, or otherwise circulated, without the publisher's prior consent, in any form of binding or cover other than that in which it is published.

*To my wife Arpita, who has been
extremely supportive in my life*

Contents

Introduction   *ix*

1. Nirvana from Faith   1
2. Nirvana from Mind   18
3. Nirvana from Emotions   28
4. Nirvana Through Self-development   40
5. Nirvana Through Equanimity   55
6. Nirvana Through Four Noble Truths   66

Acknowledgements   77

Introduction

In the beginning, man was only slightly better than the rest of Creation. In fact, man was not half as strong as the mightiest creatures on land or sea. However, man's distinctive power of thought and an inquisitive nature differentiated him from the rest. With the help of his mind and the power of thought, he has been able to cut through hilly terrains with an intricate network of roads that connects distinct worlds. He has been able to connect a diverse people through a smart digital network, empowered by a technological revolution. This same mind has also been instrumental in enabling man to walk on the moon and dream of lands far beyond the realms of this mortal world, and embark on a quest for outer space to establish himself as the dominant species in this universe.

Yet it is the same mind that man has been unable to conquer and guide; that creates obstacles in his union with nature and the diversity within the universe. Consciousness is an aspect of the mind that has enabled man to develop qualities like subjectivity, sentience and the ability to distinguish between oneself and one's environment. Thus it has helped man to start thinking.

Actions Follow Thoughts

Our actions are the outcomes of our thoughts. Man's power to think has enabled him to create innovations that help the entire human race. Our thoughts have helped us evolve and progress. They have helped us sustain and create new life. Yet, it is also the negative, impatient power unleashed by restless thoughts in agitated minds that has caused the chaos and confusion we see all around us—violence, environmental degradation, terrorism, disease, sorrows and suffering. Just as our power of critical thinking helps us, conversely, it is also the power of the toxic thoughts—anger, guilt, fear, insecurity, revenge and anxiety—that slowly poisons the mind and the body, which is man's undoing. Man has created elements of both creation and destruction with the help of his powerful mind. On one hand he aspires to research outer space; on the other, he aspires to put weapons in space.

Unforgiving and harmful ideas flit between the extreme ends of the thought spectrum, from love to hate, from anger to calm, desperately seeking balance. This apparent 'truth' of cosmic duality motivates us to look beyond the chaos and the confusion to those fleeting moments of calm, as man yearns for 'Oneness'—the moment when time and space merge and nothing else matters. When we feel one with everything around us and experience inner peace. A union between man and nature—oneness with the universe.

Let us imagine a situation—on a rainy day, a passing car splashes muddy water on us. Our natural reaction is annoyance, and even anger, at the unknown stranger. Can we reverse time with our anger and make the incident not happen? Absolutely not. We simply cannot turn around time and undo the action already taken or rectify the situation. Humans have not yet come up with a tool to manipulate time. Despite being unable to create any impact through our anger, we still tend to hold these negative emotions within us for long periods of time. Alternatively, if our mind is calm, we may simply ignore the event. The same mind can think and react in two opposite ways to the same situation. Why do we get angry or display other negative emotions? We tend to get angry when our mind feels threatened or attacked, or it gets the impression that people do not respect our feelings or possessions. We get angry when things do not go as planned, or if we feel sidelined or suppressed. Everyone has their own triggers for what makes them angry.

Now consider a situation such as the 9/11 attacks. Can you possibly imagine any individual carrying out such a heinous attack if he had control over his mind? Just like our mind can create, it also possesses immense power to destroy whatever it has built. Taking charge of the mind involves applying a filter on all thoughts that come to the mind. The stronger the filter is, the calmer and more composed the mind is. No thought—including the impulsive ones—can materialize without the approval of the conscious mind. We produce 60,000-80,000 thoughts per day, and 2,500-3,000 thoughts per hour.[1] The human brain finds it difficult to process all of them, and selectively picks up the thoughts that are essential or matter to us the most. Controlling the mind means focusing on some of these thoughts and letting go of others, which may not benefit us and may end up harming others instead.

Letting Go of Disruptive Thoughts

The great sages, in order to tame their minds, retreat from the world, as they want to let go of the distractions that initially occupied their minds when they set out to find certain specific answers. In order to come up with a solution to a problem, we need to let go of everything but the problem at hand.

Why do we need to take charge of our mind? The mind is nothing but a powerhouse of desires and thoughts that can be positive, negative or neutral. The final nature of the mind is the aggregate of the positive, negative and neutral thoughts that we have. The mind is naturally wary. In order to keep us alive, it takes decisions almost instantaneously. The dependency of the body on the mind for these natural instincts tends to make the mind bossy.

---

[1] https://www.huffpost.com/entry/healthy-relationships_b_3307916

The fact that we consider the mind to be the ultimate decision maker in our lives, in all situations, has made it exert absolute control over almost everything we do. Simply put, our mind tends to control our body, if we do not make the effort to control the former. As a result, we become what our mind wants us to become—its slave—and once we become a slave of our desires, morality and ethics disappear.

> *Life is one big road with lots of signs*
> *So when you riding through the ruts*
> *Don't complicate your mind*
> *Flee from hate, mischief and jealousy!*
> *Don't bury your thoughts*
> *Put your vision to reality, yeah!*
> *Wake Up and Live!*
>
> —Bob Marley

These words convey the same message—that of taking charge of the mind. Having a proper vision of the future, coupled with the desire and dedication to work towards it, results in success. Is it possible to achieve any goal if we don't strive for it with complete focus? The answer is a clear no.

Imagine a cricket world cup match between India and Pakistan, with thousands of fans cheering the teams on both sides. In such a situation, it is extremely easy for a player to have a lapse in concentration and for the team to end up losing the game. Sometimes, even a lapse of a second may change the entire dynamics of the match. It is this one second that might define the outcome of all major moments in our lives. A cricketer who is focusing on an incoming ball may move his eye to look at the excited crowd for a split second, costing the team a wicket. In a game, several activities occur simultaneously, and a lot of practice is needed for a mind to focus on the most important elements and differentiate them from others which can be safely termed as 'distractions'—thoughts or actions that hold a certain attraction but may result in negative outcomes.

Prince Arjuna and his brothers were once asked by their guru, Dronacharya, to shoot the eye of a bird perched on a tree, with a bow and arrow. Each of the brothers was given the bow in turn, but before they could shoot, each of them was asked the same question—'what do you see?' All of them, except for Arjuna, described the entire scene in front of them, and none of them was allowed to shoot. Arjuna, on the other hand, said that he could only see the eye of the bird. Guru Dronacharya was impressed and allowed Arjuna to shoot, and the arrow hit its mark. The conscious mind of Arjuna was able to distinguish between the essential and non-essential elements in the whole scene in front of him, and he focused on only the essential aspect, which was necessary for achieving his goal. His mind simply restricted the range of his visibility to the eye of the bird. All other visual information was immaterial, and he decided to let it go.

Nirvana is a state in which we have no thoughts, no desires, and no suffering, yet possess complete knowledge; it is a state of no feelings in which we are devoid of emotions, yet have a firm sense of our surroundings. It is a state in which the mind is free, alert and calm at the same time—at peace and in equilibrium with the surroundings. Nirvana is like being in free fall. The mind flows freely, with no sign of control. We have no sense of time and space, yet there is an understanding that we are divinely guided. It is a sense of being driven towards a greater purpose than ours, and a seemingly innate realization of what is real and what is unreal. It ensures that we see the shallowness of worldly desires and begin to achieve a sense of union with the universe.

The root of all suffering is attachment. We feel so attached to certain things that their absence makes us develop negative emotions. Everything in this world is perishable and destroyable. Matter changes form. Yet we feel attached to things that are transient, that would not sustain themselves—and ourselves with them—for long. Nirvana is attaining the intelligence to associate with something greater than us, which is not perishable and which can give us an ultimate sense of fulfilment. We need to attain Nirvana to vibrate at the same frequency as the universe, thus achieving a sense of oneness with it.

In the context of Buddhism and Jainism, the meaning of Nirvana is interpreted slightly differently. According to the texts of these religions, Nirvana is the highest possible attainment in the life of an individual, and a state of mind wherein all pain, hatred, greed, desire etc. melt and dissolve. Nirvana leads to Moksha.

Moksha is a concept in Hinduism which means freedom from the cycle of life and death. Right from our birth, we are chained to our deeds and thus experience the sorrow of parting from the things that define us. Moksha is liberation from all sorrows and escape from the harsh realities of life, which is full of them. The way to attain Moksha is to realize the ultimate truth—that the human soul is a part of something larger. This realization prevents us from entering the cycle of reincarnation and subjecting ourselves to the inevitable suffering that accompanies each birth and subsequent journey of life.

The word 'Nirvana' is comprised of two words: 'Nir', meaning 'out', and 'Vana', meaning 'blown'. In the literal sense, the word thus means 'blown out', or in other words, extinguishing the desire to keep burning—that is, the cycle of life. It is important to note that the word 'Nirvana' is not mentioned in the Vedas and the Upanishads and must have been added later, with the advent of Buddhism. The word is interpreted differently in the context of Hindusim, where it is associated with attaining the Lord.

This book is not a discourse on religion, but an effort to understand Nirvana for the betterment of our daily lives. It is my belief that by following the principles of Nirvana, one can lead a more balanced life. This, in turn, is the key to attaining both personal and professional bliss.

Have you ever seen a successful person who is unhappy and filled with negative emotions frequently? A person whose life is a success story is a person who has replaced the negative aspects of his mind with positive ones and thus lives in utmost happiness and fulfilment. In these fast-paced modern times, perhaps it is time for us to pause, take a small break and delve deep within ourselves to find the true meaning and purpose of our lives. This book is a small attempt in this regard. It is intended to be useful not just to professionals and students, but to all individuals, irrespective of their faith or community. The book is divided into six sections, focused on what to do and what not to do to achieve Nirvana, which will in turn help us lead better lives. Nirvana is not achieved just by following the scriptures—it happens when the desire to attain it vanishes. It happens when we feel we are already in a state of Nirvana.

1
Nirvana from Faith

Bodhisattva is enlightened in the Buddhist philosophy, religion, tradition. He's enlightened. It's fine—I don't really fight it—but many people use the term 'zen' and terms like 'Nirvana,' 'enlightenment' in an almost superficial way. It's not that complicated.

—Edgar Ramirez, Venezuelan actor and winner of Cesar Award for Most Promising Actor in 2011

'Nirvana' is often conflated with our respective faiths—namely Hinduism, Buddhism and Jainism. It is true that its origins can be found in religious scriptures, yet attaining Nirvana has no relation to one's religion or faith. Religions are basically historical and cultural systems followed by specific groups of people for generations, which evolve with time. Faith, on the other hand, is a personal feeling of an individual. If 'Nirvana' is associated with these particular religions, then does it imply that followers of other religions like Christianity and Islam cannot attain it? It is quite possible that man may already have, quietly and unknowingly, experienced the state of Nirvana before it officially became as an elusive concept and an integral part of Buddhism.

Religion Is Just a Path

It seems that all religions have two parts: 'Purpose' and 'Path'. In terms of purpose, all religions are the same. They all teach us to follow and carry forth the message of love, compassion, self-discipline and contentment. It is in terms of path that the message may be interpreted differently.

All religions have the same set of values and principles; therefore, it is futile to compare them, as the destination is the same. Some readers might protest that this is inherently not true, as Christianity and Islam do not believe in the concept of rebirth, unlike Hinduism and Jainism. However, it is important to consider this apparent dissimilarity from another perspective—that all of these religions prescribe the performance of good deeds throughout one's lifetime. They all stress on the importance of service to others. Is there, then, any significant difference? All of these ideologies define service to others as an ultimate deed. This service is, in fact, a path to Nirvana.

While all may agree that it is important to contribute towards the betterment of society, few realize that this alone can relieve us from pain and suffering, as we focus on making a positive difference. Imagine that you are an extremely rich person with twenty palatial houses. Now, think for a moment—you can only live in one of the houses. So instead of buying nineteen other properties, it would have been much better to spend some of the wealth on educating or building houses for homeless people. Greed has no limit. 'Use things; love people' should be the central mantra of our lives.

It is extremely important to view religions as nothing more than paths to follow in life. Our religion is often determined by our birth, but our faith is chosen by us. In this context, 'Nirvana', too, is another path that can be chosen by us.

The origin of Nirvana in Buddhism happened when Prince Siddhartha, relinquishing his worldly possessions, sat and meditated under the Bodhi tree—thus unravelling the ultimate truth and attaining enlightenment, along with the name 'Gautama Buddha'. But long before Buddha understood the concept of Nirvana and attained it, the ascetic people of India knew of ways to attain the final liberation. They had different names for it, of which Nirvana is one. Buddha suggested that attaining Nirvana is attaining a state of peace and happiness that arises due to the lack of desires, of seeking and striving. The Vedic tradition divided human life into four segments: Brahmacharya (age of seeking knowledge; practising celibacy), Grihasta (settling down with a life partner and starting a family), Vanaprastha (living in the middle of nature; the life of a forest dweller) and Sanyasa (renunciation of worldly desires). It was customary that humans had to give up the use of fire during the period of Sanyasa, thus extinguishing all the fires of the body—the fires of desire, illusion, lust, greed, envy, hatred etc. Once all the fires were extinguished, one would attain Stithibutha (a state of calmness wherein one is able to control the mind and senses).

Four Seals of Buddhism

Buddhism talks of four seals that are fundamental to the religion. The four dharma seals are the four characteristics which reflect true Buddhist teachings. If all the four seals can be found in a single path or philosophy, it can be considered the path of Buddha. In many ways, I personally feel that these four seals are vital in understanding the meaning and purpose of Nirvana. The four seals are as follows:

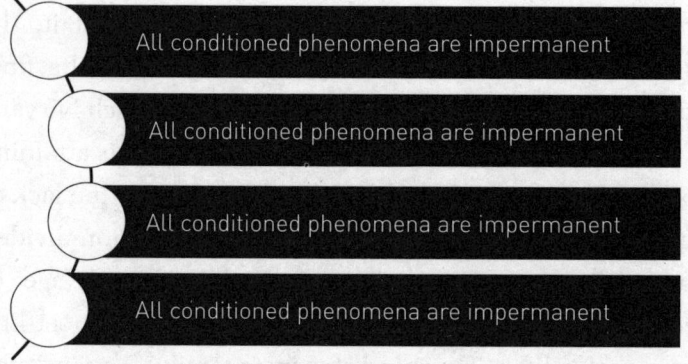

Figure 1: Four seals of Buddhism

All the physical and mental phenomena in the world are conditioned things, transient and perishable. Since these conditioned things are not real, they are not reliable sources of pleasure and are impermanent. It is the ignorance of this impermanence that results in all our suffering. It is worth noting here the importance being given to the manner in which we perceive our surroundings. That is to say, we are able to identify an object only because we associate certain qualities with it. For example, we are able to identify a food item as being sweet or spicy by relating its taste to other items. Here, we are able to distinguish it from other food items on the basis of the characteristic of taste. Discrimination is, in fact, an intellectual function emanating from comparison. If we simply look at a product sans our opinion about it, it will appear to be empty. It is our emotions regarding the product, negative or positive, that cause pain or happiness within us. It is our interpretation of events and experiences that gives rise to negative thoughts and becomes an obstacle in the realization of Nirvana. However, when we are able to judge events unfolding around us independently, without emotions, then we can certainly attain peace.

Ego Identification As the Source of Negative Thoughts

To interpret a certain event or experience and understand its significance in our lives, we need to widen the boundaries of identification. This process is hampered by our 'ego'. The ego restricts our field of judgement because of certain preconceived notions that are too rigid to be done away with. Hence, we develop intolerance to alternatives. For example, terrorism is born out of intolerance towards people holding a different set of beliefs. It is the ego of the terrorists that stops them from interpreting the truth and restricts their judgemental capacities to a narrow range. There is less room for positive thoughts to flow in when ego occupies the decision-making area of the mind.

Most negative emotions result from four kinds of thoughts and feelings we tend to have: 1) a feeling that events are permanent in nature, 2) comprehending the untrue as true, 3) a belief that objects and events are self-existing and 4) the view that material objects are a source of happiness.

These ideas clearly reflect that our focus is on the outer world rather than on the betterment of our inner selves, which is the source of negative thoughts. We often tend to be driven by the intricacies of how people perceive us rather than the idea of being our true selves. Your persona is the way you present yourself to the world and the character traits you allow others to see. We shape our persona based on how we want the world to see us. For instance, others expect us to be wealthy, glamourous and good-looking. Today, one's actions are guided by others' expectations of them, rather than by being in the moment. This belief system can be debilitating to our personal growth, as we will forever be chasing material pursuits.

Greed and desire often drive us to take shortcuts to success instead of focusing on the journey and discovering knowledge in the process. For example, when an individual focuses on accumulating wealth, he forgets to enjoy the true meaning of life—which is finding fulfilment, rather than indulging one's greed for more wealth. Beyond a point, further addition of wealth has no real purpose. Would you like to earn an additional one million USD, or spend time with your kids? None of us are going to live forever; our desires have limited purpose and serve no one beyond a point. We often think that if we were celebrities, our lives would be different. However, are we also willing to make the journey they have made to succeed? Are we willing to compromise on our values and ethics to reach stardom? Will we really have any peace if we undertake such a path?

Income disparity between individuals is clearly one of the major causes of conflict in the world. While some individuals can afford a luxurious lifestyle, others are going without food. This huge gap in income has led to varied levels of contentment among people. The poor keep on desiring the lives of the rich. The rich compare themselves with the richer and feel the need to reach their level. Desire has a higher growth rate than life expectancy. We want too many things in life within too small a span of time. For example, suppose a woman who has struggled with poverty throughout her life gets a marriage proposal from a rich man. She immediately says yes, feeling that all her lifelong desires, accumulated over her struggling years, will now be fulfilled. She gets married and starts experiencing luxuries and finds happiness—until she gets bored of her current state of life. There is always a point when the joy we derive from something plateaus, and the thing ceases to give us happiness. Once we have enjoyed it for long enough, our mind jumps to the next big thing in line. The woman looks up and starts comparing herself to others who enjoy greater luxury. The journey is endless. We can never attain a full stop to our list of desires. When we feel like we have fulfilled a desire, the desire transforms itself—it evolves into something else. There is no way to reach an ultimate level of satiety, if we keep fuelling the fire of desire. We can control our desires only when we understand the transient nature of the world around us. The same philosophy is outlined in the Bhagavad Gita, which also talks about giving up our desires in order to attain oneness with the universe.

Self-knowledge for Oneness

Desire is an emotion, a strong feeling in response to some circumstance or stimulus—past, present or future—that drives us by powerfully influencing our thoughts and behaviours, and can even cause chemical changes in our bodies. It is so all-pervasive that whenever we try to perceive an object, we attach emotions to it. These emotions make us either want to possess the object, or despise it. In light of this power of emotions, if we consider the extremism and terrorism around us, we will see that these are fuelled by the emotions of intolerance and hatred. As emotional beings, how can we attain peace? Peace can only be attained once we gain knowledge of the self and understand the nature of our mind, from which the emotions emanate.

It is a choice that all of us must make—whether we wish to promote positive emotions in our mind or be driven by the negativity around us. If we can, instead, create feelings of compassion and care in our minds, we can build a sense of belonging to the world around us. This will help to create a sense of positivity while also building our inner qualities for the betterment of lives around us. Developing positive feelings within us moulds us to undertake constructive actions that benefit others. When we consider our surroundings as a part of our self, questions of morality and ethics do not arise, as we consider ourselves part of the universe and not separate entities. Everything around us is our own, and it is our innate nature, as humans, to do everything possible for the betterment and enhancement of all that is ours or that we are a part of. In other words, we tend to stop seeing ourselves as different from each other, thereby achieving a sense of union with nature. When we feel neither an attachment to worldly objects nor an aversion to them, we are closer to Nirvana. As all of creation is the product of the experiments of nature, integrating ourselves into our creator (Mother Nature) helps in achieving perfect union with the universe. Meditation, too, is prescribed as a tool to take charge of the mind, with increased awareness of our connection to those around us. This state of being connected, or being at one with everything around us, is known as Nirvana.

Meditation vs Analytical Meditation

While these are the keys to the state of Nirvana as provided in Buddhism, the teachings of Buddha always urge us to question them and not accept anything on blind faith. I admire this quality of Buddhism that promotes scepticism and asks us to perform analytical meditation in order to discover the truth.

I would like to decipher the difference that analytical meditation promotes as compared to the regular meditation that most of us undertake. In regular meditation, we tend to close our eyes and keep our mind free of all thoughts for the time being. In case of analytical meditation, however, we tend to focus on an issue and tune our attention to it. Consider a situation where you have a doubt about a decision you must take. In such a scenario, analytical meditation can be extremely helpful in getting a clearer picture of reality. Analytical meditation does not tell you to become free from worldly affairs—rather, it inspires you to conduct them with greater conviction. It is through such conviction that an individual can also attain mental transformation. Our brains are wired to react to anything uncertain with fear. As the level of uncertainty increases, the brain shifts control to the limbic system, where negative emotions like anxiety and panic are generated. Once a person is convinced that the result of this uncertainty is a desirable outcome and starts believing in it as if he or she has already seen the future unfolding, the negative emotions disappear. There is a chemical shift in the brain suggesting that the outcome is known, and the mind is filled with positive emotions like happiness.

If we consider the human brain as a research and development (R&D) lab experimenting with various emotions in response to various thoughts, we can see that it is a combination of these emotions that defines our mood at any given moment. Each combination can create infinite hues of emotion. For example, when it comes to practising a faith in a country like ours, individuals can be quite vocal and tend to act in an irrational manner. In such a scenario, would it not be more beneficial for the person to use his or her intelligence, together with analytical meditation, to create a more reasonable response?

It is often said that our brain and our heart behave differently. Emotional sentiments and responses are thought to figuratively originate from the heart, whereas rational or logical thinking is believed to emerge from the brain. The heart and the brain may not always agree. For example, the heart may want to eat sweets but the brain may prohibit it as you have diabetes. At times, it is extremely difficult to connect with either of them, and at other times, both may seem correct. However, it is through analytical meditation

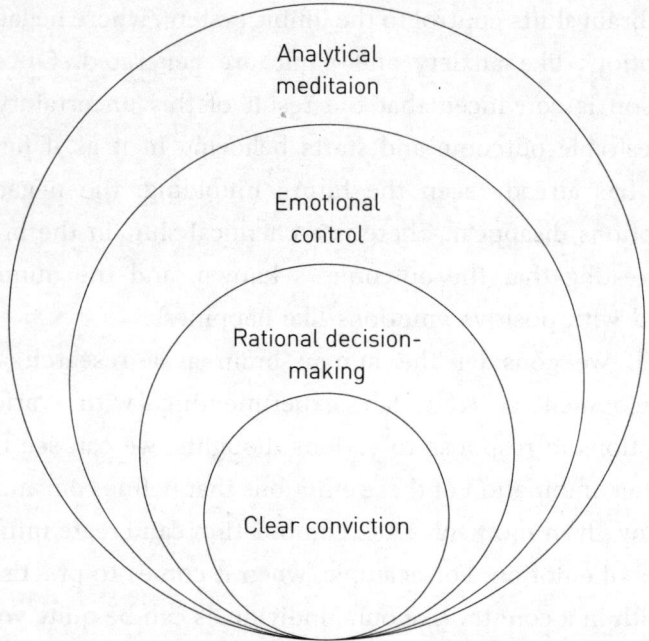

Figure 2: Benefits of analytical meditation

that we can achieve union between them. The brain and heart can work together and lead to much better decision-making.

For instance, religion, prescribing rules of conduct, forms our 'brain thoughts', which are a preconceived set of rules followed and carried forward through generations. Faith is a 'heart thought', which is the result of our own choice. It is what we choose to follow. While I do not question the mindset of those who follow religious scriptures or leaders blindly without question, does it really build a sense of conviction? Our intellect and our experiences work together in such situations. For instance, an age-old custom might have been followed in olden times because of some science behind it. It might have been a solution to a major crisis at that time. Over the ages, humans began following it blindly. Now the crisis is over, but the custom is still carried forward through generations, as no one has ever questioned it. No one has thought that the custom may not be of any use at present. Day by day man grows wiser. He encounters new problems and devises new solutions for them. The experiences of a lifetime are passed on to the next generation, which subsequently builds new experiences after further introspection. All these experiences, combined with human intellect, give birth to innovation. For example, fire was once considered by cavemen to be the wrath of the spirits of nature, until humans discovered the art of making fire. That experience got carried forward through several generations until man developed the art of taming fire. Now fire is used in various parts of religious worship. This is how our belief systems transformed the fear of fire into the conviction of mastering it.

Analytical Meditation As a Tool for Nirvana

When we focus on only two aspects of meditation, desire and pain, then our sufferings continue to increase. Pain is an effect of not having what one wants or having what one does not want. Nonfulfillment of desire causes pain.

We suffer when we are not pleased with our current role in this universe. We constantly complain and ask the universe for more, sending waves of unhappiness to it. But the universe, in life, is a magnifying mirror. The arrows of negativity shot at it are sent back amplified, causing further discontentment. Thus pain leads to further desire and desire leads to more pain, and the cycle continues. However, if we focus on the removal of desire and on achieving ultimate peace, then we are able to guide ourselves towards attaining this peace. This is based on the principle that whatever we focus on is amplified!

The reason Buddhism asks us to meditate on our suffering is because analytical meditation will enable us to find an alternative to the suffering. We will be able to understand the transient nature of our suffering and find a way to resolve it. But if we are unable to find the way, we will continue to suffer. In such a scenario, compassion and love need to become the sole purposes of our lives. When we begin to focus on giving rather than expecting things from others, it fuels our compassion. When we expect something, we fuel our desire; by eliminating our expectations, we eliminate our desires and thereby end our suffering. This is true for the entire human race and for followers of any faith, as the basic principles outlined in any religion are the same. If we cultivate positive feelings in our mind, we tend to build an inner circle of positive energy around us. If we practise true compassion and caring for others, we can build a sense of positive human values. This creates a sense of positivity and inner peace not just for the individual, but for humanity in general.

Every religion lays importance on prayers and dedication to God. Some religions also lay importance on the value of sacrifice for attaining God. However, no matter how much we pray, true peace and union with God can only be attained through service. Often, individuals say that they are committed to performing their duties; but fail at the point of action. They either become complacent or too lethargic to perform the action with the required level of diligence and effort. For example, if an exam requires one to study for ten hours a day, a person cannot expect to pass by studying for just one or two hours. Such an individual cannot attain Nirvana.

In order to attain Nirvana, we need to be consistent in our efforts. Just like an exam cannot be passed by studying for just a couple of hours, helping someone once won't lead us to peace. It is only through compassion for others—with unflinching trust and on a constant basis—that one can open the doors to Nirvana. Just as companies have a corporate social responsibility (CSR), individuals, too, have an individual social responsibility (ISR). It is important to understand which set of issues motivate us to do our bit for society.

How can this action be made possible? The first step is to be clear about our goal and vision. If, as individuals, we understand our purpose in life, we can take the proper steps to attain it. For example, a doctor has a choice to treat patients as his or her means of livelihood; but the same doctor has a moral obligation to treat those who cannot afford the treatment, out of compassion. If we do not have a clear goal, then we will deviate and end up taking a zigzag path which will only cause mayhem in our lives.

As individuals, we have our respective religious beliefs. They all prescribe different paths—each leading to the almighty. Some might believe in rebirth, whereas others might believe in a single life. Some might believe in fasting, whereas others might prescribe ahimsa or non-violence towards all creatures. There is, however, one thing that is at the core of every religion: attainment of peace. If, as individuals, we only strive for our own survival, our own growth and our desires, and lead individualistic lives, will there be any difference between us and other animals? Humans have been given the gift of intelligence to be able to make a positive difference. Our time on Earth can be looked at as a vacation. Just as a vacation lasts for a limited number of days, our time on Earth is also limited.

We have a choice in front of us—whether to look for pleasure or seek peace. In our quest to attain pleasure, we will harbour feelings of greed. This, in turn, will deter us from the moral path and make us commit sins. It will eventually lead to the destruction of our mental peace. On the other hand, if we prevent such desires from impacting us and consider all creation as equal, we can retain our mental peace. All religions teach us to pursue the path of humanity and help those in need. It has repeatedly been indicated as the key to attaining peace. So the path to attaining Nirvana through religion lies in the service to others. In case an individual is unable to help others, he should at least not be a cause of pain to them.

Food for thought:

In order to build a world of peace, we must ensure that we do our bit in removing disparities among various sections. What are the areas you can contribute in, to achieve this goal?

2

Nirvana from Mind

The extinction of desire, the extinction of hatred, the extinction of illusion... The extinction of 'thirst' is Nibbāna.

—Walpola Rahula,
Buddhist monk, scholar and writer

The human mind is an extremely interesting creation. It has the power to create and destroy. In fact, just as it is said that the pen is mightier than the sword, similarly, our thoughts often determine the path or course of action that we choose for ourselves. In such situations, it becomes imperative to be able to take charge of our mind with awareness. It is simply impossible for a directionless mind to achieve peace and a state of Nirvana. While one's body can feel their surroundings through their senses, it is the connection with one's mind that helps in achieving the sense of consciousness. It is our mind that determines our response to a situation that our body experiences.

In order to keep our mind pure, we must experience a state of 'thoughtlessness'—that is, keep our mind free of all thoughts. It is extremely vital that we continue to practise meditation and experience this sense of luminosity in our minds.

When we consider the connection of our mind with our body, we realize the transient nature of the latter. We must empower our mind to understand the cycle of existence in order to be free from all pain and suffering. This can only be achieved by the destruction of all emotions, positive and negative, to achieve a sense of mental bliss. This does not mean that the 'self' is non-existent in nature. It exists, and is ever changing. The self—which consists of our idea about ourselves, the soul as our inner spirit and our mind—is what drives us to perform actions. What human beings need to realize is that the self is transient. Just like we change clothes, the self also takes on new forms at regular intervals. Just as the mind is continuous, the self is also endless.

If we further analyze the relationship of the mind and the body, we realize that the mind cannot exist without the body. When a person dies, the mind also ceases to function. However, there is a level of consciousness that remains even when we sleep. In fact, our mind can be divided into several levels, with each level having a different kind of dependence on the body. These levels indicate the varying levels of our consciousness at various points of time during the day. This is drawn largely from spiritual principles, in order to understand our mind more effectively.

Our emotions are the greatest hurdle towards attaining inner peace, as they can lead to expectations and dependency. There are two ways that one can take charge of these negative emotions: one, by not allowing such feelings to develop, and two, by understanding the impact of such emotions. If we use and programme our minds in such a manner, we can distance ourselves from negative emotions such as jealousy and hatred. Mind-programming is an extremely useful technique in steering our mind towards the right direction. Just as our body requires food to grow, our mind also requires positive thoughts and feelings to develop correctly.

In order to eliminate negative feelings, one needs to ask a few questions: What is the impact of these emotions? Are they impacting our enemies, or affecting our own health? There can be two sets of causes for emotions that overwhelm the mind: external and internal. External factors can affect our peace of mind. For example, when you do not receive a promotion that was due, it can affect your mental state and impact your calmness. However, you can either choose to allow this event and the circumstances around it to run in your mind in an endless loop—which will build up stress and affect your health—or simply learn to let go. In the stressful lives that young professionals lead, it is extremely important to focus on the tasks at hand and not on factors that we cannot control. Overthinking and over-analyzing a single event are primary causes of stress and confusion.

Being Self-centred

One major obstacle in the path of achieving Nirvana through our mind is being self-centred, which restricts our area of operation. This mental state compels us to always compare our situation to that of others who are more successful, which naturally builds feelings of inadequacy within us. Our problems become magnified. Conversely, if we broaden our horizons and become inclusive by considering everyone as part of one family, our problems appear small—as tiny as a speck in the vast universe. We then realize that there are others with problems much larger than our own. We realize that it is our inherent duty to be of service to others. Our problems as individuals become insignificant and we begin to realize the importance of helping others. Christianity says that when Lord Jesus was describing the final judgement that will take place at the end of the world, he said, 'As long as you did something for the least of my brothers, you did it for me.' He clearly implied that helping any individual is the same as being of service to the entirety of humanity. This service can be in the form of feeding someone, giving water to the thirsty or even providing shelter. Any act performed as charity, without any expectations, can be considered a service to humanity.

When we decide to help others, we have already decided to change the world for the better. We may never meet the person we help, but we are building a sphere of positive energy around ourselves. It makes us feel good about ourselves. It relieves us from stress. Our inability to manage stress in our personal life often creates a desire to escape from it. In such scenarios, substances like alcohol or drugs offer quick relief by creating a feeling of numbness within us. For a brief period, they make everything around us seem perfectly normal. This eventually leads to addiction, as we fail to manage our lives without these substances. We lose the courage to face our hurdles and instead try to avoid and ignore them. Our mental attitude and our outlook towards problems create a major difference. A person with a positive outlook will build positive energy and create a positive atmosphere.

Being of service to others also means taking care of your own family. There is no practical difference, as they are also part of creation. However, when care is extended exclusively to one's own family, then it amounts to selfishness. Just like we pray for our family, we also need to pray for everyone around us, including our neighbours, if we wish to live a peaceful life with a happy mind.

The role of teachers is also equally important. Students should be taught these basic human values at an early age. Just as we teach the distinction between good and evil, it is equally important to teach the value of service. This can be done not just through words, but also through actions.

Students need to be taught the value of compassion and the importance of being kind.

Another important way of getting closer to a state of Nirvana by taking charge of the mind is to develop the awareness to resolve issues through dialogue. It is common to have conflicts and differences of opinion, and healthy dialogue is a much-needed path towards resolving these issues (and subsequently, Nirvana) without creating negative feelings.

As we age, our body decays but our mind becomes wiser. It learns to differentiate between right and wrong and act accordingly. If you compare the way you used to think ten years ago with how you think today, you will notice a significant change. It does not matter how big the change is, as long as it is positive. The transformation of the human mind can be achieved by understanding a few simple steps:

Change is sometimes slow: Just like Rome was not built in a single day, the mind cannot be transformed in a single moment. It takes years of practise and dedication, focused on a single goal. Even if the change is minimal and not dramatic, it should be considered positively, as long it occurs. In times of adversity, when all hope seems lost, we must not give up. We must retain our faith. Even if our efforts are not complete in one life, our good deeds will be carried forward to the next until we attain our goal.

Do not count the hours and days: In pursuit of a clear direction and a focused mind, it is important that we are not driven by the time that we spend in achieving it. If we do not enjoy an activity, spending long hours performing it might not provide the required results. For example, an individual who wishes to pursue photography or sports as a career might not be inclined to study engineering. Even if he studies, his mind will continue to think about a sports match or the photographs that he can click. Instead, the focus should be on the progress made. It is important to study and analyze our life's journey to find the path that is best suited for us. It is only by questioning and analyzing that we can discover the correct path.

Equality of faith: It is equally important to accept every religion and understand that their tenets are the same. Gautama Buddha, before starting his own religion, was born a Hindu. In his teachings, he accepted certain Hindu principles like Samadhi (a state of meditative consciousness) and Vipassana (understanding the human soul and the transient nature of life). We must learn to accept and have an open heart towards others.

Emotions are important: It is extremely important to recognize the importance of emotions in our lives. Without emotions, our lives will be lacklustre. There will be no meaning to events if we cannot react to them appropriately. Imagine our cricket team winning the world cup—it is natural for us to react with joy. However, it is equally important to understand the negative impact of emotions. Sometimes, emotions may look colourful in the short run, but become destructive in the long run. For example, a student, overcome by a fear of failure, decides to cheat in an exam and pass. In the short run, his objective has been fulfilled, but in the long run he has led himself to a path of ruin. Sometimes when we deviate from the correct path, there is still time for course-correction. Consider the example of Alfred Bernhard Nobel, the Swedish businessman and philanthropist who decided to give up his life's earnings that he had accrued through his invention of dynamite to set up the Nobel Prize, to be awarded every year to those with outstanding achievements in the fields of science, economics and art. The realization that he had, about using his wealth for the greater good, was a wonderful way of redeeming himself. Is this not Nirvana? Is this not the purpose of the human life?

Focus cannot be lost: All of us are born with at least one talent, if not more. Yet, most of us let it go waste. We try to find pleasure in doing things that may not be our forte. It is, therefore, extremely important to identify our life's goal and purpose early on. For example, we often look at the success of top-level athletes with awe and envy, yet ignore the years of effort that they have put in to get to that level. Is it possible for any individual to focus on something unless they have real interest in the activity? Absolutely not. Just like a top-level athlete understands his duties, every individual should know his responsibilities. This emotion is largely positive and drives us towards our goal.

It is extremely important to be able to distinguish between positive and negative emotions. While all of us experience highs and lows, one of the side effects of our fast-track lives is depression, which is becoming increasingly common in our times. Often, when the feeling of being low starts to settle in, depression becomes a constant part of our lives. It is important to talk about it with others and take whatever help is necessary. Even celebrities are opening up about the depression that they go through. The major reasons for depression are attachment, deep thinking and overanalysing a situation. This, in turn, builds up unnecessary stress and impacts us negatively. It is therefore extremely important to regularly calm ourselves and consider the world as one entity by focusing on positive events.

Human beings are complicated. Our intelligence has enabled us to create all the comforts that the world can offer, such as lavish houses, recreation centres and gadgets of all kind. We also have thousands of years of recorded history that we can refer to every now and then. All this makes us much more intelligent than the rest of creation. However, constantly demanding more from life increases our expectations, as we worry a lot more. These negative emotions cannot be destroyed even by accruing all the material comforts of life, but can definitely be reduced by focusing on a life of compassion for others. When one is mentally prepared, he or she can face any amount of physical discomfort. All sensory experiences that we face lie much below the happiness that we can achieve at the emotional level. Our sensory experiences are based on our attachment to worldly affairs, whereas our experiences at the level of emotion are based on our connection to the soul. Our mental peace can be destroyed largely because of the negative emotions that we continue to harbour in our minds.

All of us want to be happy. Any factor that brings about happiness in us can be construed as positive, whereas anything that causes stress can be viewed as negative. It is extremely important to remember that having a healthy and positive mindset is critical for a healthy life. If our mind is not healthy and always perplexed, how can we attain peace? Just like a healthy body is important, so is having a positive mind, in order to attain Nirvana.

Food for thought:

List five things that build negative emotions in you. Now list the actions you can take to let go of these emotions.

3

Nirvana from Emotions

Your emotions are the slaves to your thoughts, and you are the slave to your emotions.

—Elizabeth Gilbert, American author

Just like a picture without colour looks dull, our lives without emotions will appear dismal. Emotions can be both positive and negative. While positive emotions, like love, happiness and compassion need to be encouraged, negative emotions like fear, anger, anxiety and loneliness, that make us feel miserable, sad or vengeful must be annulled and ignored as well. This chapter focuses on how one can attain peace of mind or Nirvana by easing out of negative emotions. A man who is focused on rage and negativity can never attain peace. Our awareness of our surroundings and the events in our lives determine our reactions towards them. When positive events happen, we react positively. However, it is when negative events happen that we need to control our reactions.

The first step to overcoming negative emotions is by analysing the short-term and long-term impact of the emotions. Imagine this situation: Suresh is a young IT company salesman. In order to get a particular contract, Suresh agrees to pay a bribe to an official. His company successfully bags the contract. Suresh is widely praised by his seniors and earns himself a promotion. Years later, an investigation is launched, and Suresh is found guilty and punished as per the law, along with his company and its promoters. He loses his credibility, respect and reputation before his professional peers, family and friends.

Each of us has faced similar conflicts in our daily life. In fact, it is easy to place ourselves in Suresh's shoes for a moment and try to align his thinking to the right path. Was it not his duty to bid fairly for the contract and compete on fair terms? If he was selling a good product, was it necessary to undertake unethical means and shortcuts to success? Did it eventually serve any purpose?

A real-life example in this regard was the economic recession of 2008, when markets all around the world crashed and led to the bankruptcy of some of the oldest financial institutions. In a bid to increase profitability, exotic products and multi-level derivative options began to be traded. These were deeply related to the housing bubble, and when housing prices started to fall, it led to the creation of toxic assets. Since the assets were securitised manifold, hardly any financial institution was unaffected by this. Even legacy financial institutions such as Barings Bank and Lehman Brothers were forced to file for bankruptcy. Thousands of people became jobless overnight. The realization that shortcuts and short-term success can never go a long way should enable us to change our thinking and make the path of righteousness our goal in life.

It is extremely vital to understand the reason behind our emotions if we intend to get rid of our negativity. This is possible by seeking a cause and effect relationship in the events that have led to a negative thought pattern running like an endless loop in your mind and robbing you of inner peace. In case of any event or effect, there can be several factors leading up to it. Some of these factors are within our control, whereas others lie outside our power. This is known as the two-factor model. If we can use our intelligence to analyse and focus on the factors that are within our control, it can provide us the desired results. All of us aim for a particular outcome in a given event— instead of worrying about the outcome, we should instead direct our energy towards the effort of achieving the outcome. Awareness followed by an analysis of the cause of the negativity can help us take charge of the situation by correcting our behaviour or taking necessary action. Thus, the process can help motivate us to address the situation that has led to the problem. This will also help us to restrain our emotions from spilling out negatively towards others. On the other hand, factors which are beyond our control should spur us to either move out of the negative situation, or accept it, or simply attribute the incident to fate without overthinking, and let go.

When we build up negative emotions towards another person, we tend to believe that the other person feels similarly towards us. This, in turn, leads to a state of suspicion, wherein we attribute negative intentions to even innocuous actions by the other person, and the situation spirals, thereby actually creating mutual distrust. This way, the law of attraction—that which we focus on—is amplified. It ensures that we create situations that confirm our suspicions, which eventually become a part of our belief system. Suspicion is one of the root causes of divorce and separation. What often begins as simple suspicion eventually leads to a person performing acts out of desperation. This can include indulging in activities such as gambling or drinking, or having an affair in order to seek revenge. On the other hand, if we focus on communicating clearly with the other person and conveying our ideas rationally, the thought process underlying the negative spiral can be nipped in the bud and a healthy relationship can be built. This is especially true in workplaces. It is common to see individuals in a workplace gossiping and harbouring mistrust or jealousy towards each other. This, in turn, makes them feel lonely and depressed. It is almost like piling tonnes of garbage on oneself. Instead, if we start treating others with compassion and love, they too reciprocate the same feelings. Is there any place then for these negative feelings?

We must also stop the blame game. When an untoward incident happens, we tend to overlook our own role in creating it. We tend to point at a particular cause, driven by our own pet conspiracy theories. Instead of trying to locate the cause deep within ourselves, we start blaming everyone around us. For example, if we fail an exam, we tend to blame the teacher without realizing that, perhaps, we had not put in the required effort while studying. This results in anger being built in our mind. If we carefully analyse these events, we will find that a number of factors are responsible for them. Similarly, when a favourable event happens, we tend to attribute it to one cause or factor. This is equally untrue. All events in our life need to be properly analysed, keeping in mind both the short-term and long-term impacts of the same. If we harbour a grudge or hatred, it only impacts our own mental and physical health. If the stress becomes too high, we might even suffer a stroke or some other medical emergency. This creates a further feeling of distrust, rather than promoting mutual respect and bonhomie. Only if we analyse an event in a proper manner are we able to calm our nerves and attend to it in the best possible way. If we are calm, our response to situations will be rational. For example, if there is an argument in office with a colleague, a rational approach will involve trying to understand the situation that led to the argument. An emotional approach, on the other hand, might lead to continuing the argument and spoiling the relationship. A rational approach leads to maintaining our calm and composure, and our inability to maintain it conversely leads to restlessness.

Just like events in the present have various causes, our reactions to them will be the cause of future events. If we promote compassion, love and respect, we will get the same from others in future. If we promote hatred, jealousy and disrespect, we should expect the same from others as well. Just as a plant is born after its seed is sowed, similarly, our lives are determined by the emotions that we decide to harvest around us. It is important to look at suffering as suffering for all humanity. We should try to consider all human beings as equal and different from one another. Just like we share the same world, we also have the same spirit and emotions. Hence, we should connect with each other without our ego impacting us. If we can achieve this union with our environment, we can curb these negative emotions.

The second stage of curbing negative emotions is through spreading the message of love and compassion. This is a common message across all religions. Let us see a few examples from various religions:

Hinduism: *'He unto whom—self-centred—grief and joy sound as one word; to whose deep-seeing eyes the clod, the marble, and the gold are one; whose equal heart holds the same gentleness for lovely and unlovely things, firm-set, well-pleased in praise and dispraise; satisfied with honour or dishonour; unto friends and unto foes alike in tolerance;*

detached from undertakings—he is named Surmounter of the Qualities!'

—Bhagavad Gita

It is quite clear that the Bhagavad Gita is preaching a message of peace here by promoting a sense of peace and tolerance. It refers to an individual's ability to treat self-centred grief and joy as equal aspects of our lives. One who treats his friends and foes with tolerance is the person having all the qualities. Such a person has complete control over his thoughts and emotions and is not impacted by external events.

Buddhism: *'He has cast away ill-will; he dwells with a heart free from ill-will; cherishing love and compassion toward all living beings, he cleanses his heart from ill-will.'*

—Lord Buddha, Eight Fold Path

It is important to keep our heart free of any form of ill feelings and have a feeling of love and compassion towards all creation. If we have love, and see the love around us, it has the power of absorbing all negative emotions. Consider the military conflict between Israel and Palestine—it is largely built out of animosity and hatred towards one another. Thousands of innocent lives are lost every year owing to this conflict. Instead, if the leaders from both sides come together for a dialogue with an open mind, the conflict can perhaps be resolved. This will spare new generations feelings of hatred towards each other.

Zoroastrianism: *'A conscientious, virtuous man can convert an enemy into a friend.'*

—Zoroaster, Hymns of Atharvan

If we promote feelings of compassion, any individual can convert an enemy into a friend. It is only through such feelings of humanity that one can destroy all forms of animosity around us.

Christianity: *'Love your enemies and care for your enemies as you would care for yourself.'*

—New Testament

Christianity, too, promotes the same feeling of universal brotherhood wherein one man is no different from another. It tells us to care for another person as we would like others to care for us.

Islam: *'Allah's Apostle said, "Beware of suspicion, for suspicion is the worst of false tales, and do not look for others' faults, and do not spy on one another..."'*

—Hadith, Bukhari Vol 8, Book 73 no. 92

Islam too seeks to promote brotherhood among humans and preaches against suspicion by asking us to overlook the faults of others.

All religions advise followers to trust each other and promote feelings of tolerance and love for one another. Terrorist outfits like the ISIS or Al-Qaeda or LTTE are the direct results of feelings of animosity. Religion is meant to hold us together, not drive us away from each other. Patience, and being content with what we have in life, are two more factors in curbing our negative emotions. When we are greedy, we tend to feel jealous and accumulate wealth only for ourselves. In such situations, if the outcome does not satisfy our greed, we tend to be extremely negative about other people. We often compare our state with others without understanding the journey that they have undertaken. For example, we can look at an achiever like Mukesh Ambani or Ratan Tata either with jealousy or with admiration and respect. If our dominant feeling is jealousy, it will not yield any result except for impacting our health and mental peace. On the other hand, if we admire them, we can drive our efforts in becoming like them one day. In such a situation, if we can be patient and content with whatever we have achieved, negative emotions can definitely be curbed. In fact, all religions teach this. Instead of pointlessly visiting religious places, we should instead focus on making these feelings and teachings part of our daily lives.

The third manner of taking charge of our negative emotions is by identifying the roots of these emotions. This involves being able to understand the various misconceptions surrounding them. It is often our misconceptions about someone that lead to them. If we can instead have a dialogue and try to find out if our analysis is correct, we can prevent many of our negative emotions. Our first misconception is identification. We often consider a non-permanent thing as permanent and an impure object as pure. We then start to experience happiness from these objects, without realizing their true nature. For example, many people attain so-called peace by consuming alcohol—choosing something that not only intoxicates them but also adversely affects their health. A man is known by the company he keeps. Therefore, we should choose our friends carefully, picking those who can guide us in making the right decisions at critical points in our lives. If we have supportive and honest friends, they will prevent us from engaging in self-destructive activities such as gambling. They will help in keeping our moral fabric strong and influence us positively at all times.

Our second misconception is of time. We do not realize the difference between permanent and temporary objects. We sometimes choose objects which do not have a lasting impact. For example, when shopping at an e-commerce website, we may find an article that is useful to us. We do not hesitate to buy it, as it provides us instant gratification. However, such feelings do not last, and over a period of time, such happiness disappears.

The third misconception is overlooking the transient nature of feelings. We often believe that our feelings and emotions are everlasting. We feel that no event will cause any change to these emotions. However, once such a feeling is reduced, negative emotions tend to take over the void.

The fourth misconception is a feeling of self-above-others. We often tend to overestimate our own importance and value in the grand scheme of things. We tend to feel that we are all-important in this world and irreplaceable. We consider ourselves superstars. We forget that just as a superstar depends on others to deliver a performance on screen, we too are dependent on others to lead a happy life.

There is no creation on this planet which is self-sufficient or self-supporting. Man is a social creation, who needs company to survive, and we are but small parts of a larger environment. The more we are able to give up on the feeling of being self-sufficient, the more we will be able to understand the value of others. It will bring about a change in our attitude, from being self-centred to one of bonhomie and mutual respect for everyone around us. The way we perceive a situation makes all the difference in our lives. When we feel gratitude for all that we have in our life, we can also feel compassion.

For example, if a tragic or unjust event happens and we think about it over and over again, negative emotions build up in our mind and body. We are filled with rage. However, if we look at the same event with the idea that something far worse could have happened, or that we were protected and came out alL right, we feel better. Rather than the event itself, it is the glass that we look at it through that makes all the difference in our lives. Just because no one has seen God, should we say that God does not exist? Instead, we can say that God exists in the mutual love and compassion for others. It is in our good actions and ability to see the good in others that God exists. If we are unable to see something, it does not mean it is not there. Just like air can only be felt, our mind and consciousness too need to be programmed and trained to only cultivate positive emotions. If we fail to imbibe such a nature, our negative emotions will eventually destroy ourselves.

Anger is, in fact, one of the seven deadly sins. Anger can often lead to the destruction of all relationships. When a person who is angry takes a decision in this state of rage, it can only destroy friendships and relationships. Such a person can never be successful in building an atmosphere of trust and love for those around him.

Individuals often look for a concrete way to achieve Nirvana. Yet there is no definite path to achieve it. We need to understand that our mind needs to be trained in order to rid ourselves of negative thoughts and emotions. Based on our own analysis, our mind will be able to understand and detect the path that is best suited for us in our quest to attain Nirvana.

Food for thought:

Sit back and relax for two minutes. Then consider all the moments in the day when you experienced a negative emotion. How would you have handled them differently, if they were viewed through love and compassion?

4
Nirvana Through Self-development

Treat a man as he is and he will remain as he is. Treat a man as he can and should be and he will become as he can and should be.

—Steven R. Covey, author

The primary difference between humans and other animals is their level of intelligence. We are able to communicate with each other, and our ability to think has led to the creation of futuristic products such as mobile phones and the internet. Human beings not only possess memory, but an ability to learn from the past and plan for the future too. We have the ability to foresee the future based on past events—for ourselves, our children and future generations. This creates a sense of belonging and a desire for a better future that is wildly different from other animals. This is also a cause for greater suffering among humans.

Intelligence: A Drawback

Our higher intelligence enables us to visualize. We have been able to build modern cities from scratch and are now looking for ways to colonize outer space. However, our desires sometimes lead us into situations where, in order to satisfy them, we take the wrong path. Corruption in public life is the result of this insatiable desire. Because of this, even a rich person desires more wealth. Even a famous person feels that he is not famous enough. Desire of this kind brings about more sorrow than happiness. It is quite common to find people in the workplace being unhappy not because they have received a low pay hike, but because someone else has received a greater hike. This power of discrimination and comparison is unique to human beings and the root cause of our suffering and unhappiness.

The other important aspects to consider are physical and mental experiences. Physical experiences refer to sensory experiences such as touch, whereas mental experiences refer to our thoughts and imaginations, which may or may not be true. Imagine an ailing old man in bed, whose body has decayed due to age. He has fulfilled all his duties and responsibilities, and though in pain, is happy. Now consider another person, extremely successful in life and physically fit as well. However, his personal life and relationships are in shambles and he does not have any friends. Who do you think will be more comfortable? In my view, being in a state of mental happiness is the key to success. Physical comforts that we bring into our lives through our wealth have no purpose unless we have attained mental happiness. It is important that our mind realizes the futile nature of gathering wealth and that the true purpose of our lives in is helping out others.

In today's materialistic world, there is no clear distinction between right and wrong. We often tend to view anything that gives us satisfaction or happiness as being right and anything that causes us pain as being wrong. In the same context, it is often seen that we construe anything that gives us more power, authority or wealth as largely positive. The teachings that we imbibe today are driven by a materialistic society, without focus on integrity and a value system. Being educated and professionally successful is definitely necessary, but not at the cost of an erosion of values. In order to determine what is intrinsically right and wrong, we need to connect with our inner feelings or thoughts when we encounter a person or a situation. We tend to respect and revere people who are successful in life. We admire Mr Ratan Tata for his contribution to Indian industry. However, if we come across a person of his age on the road, we tend to ignore them. We often tend to ignore those who are struggling and need our help. We are therefore primarily driven by a system of wealth today, unlike the social system that was prevalent in ancient India.

Under this system, each person belonged to one of four varnas or castes: Brahmins for wisdom and knowledge, Kshatriyas for warfare, Vaishnavas for trade and Shudras for menial tasks. The system was not based on birth, and if a person born in a family of Shudras acquired knowledge, he could become a Brahmin, based on his skills and qualities. It was a system based on merit and respect. For instance, some say Maharishi Valmiki was born in a family of Shudras; yet he is revered as one of the greatest saints of Hinduism. Valmiki earned his livelihood by stealing from others. However, when he realized the futile nature of this, he changed his path and wrote the Ramayana. Brahmins in that era never focused on accumulating wealth. They travelled from house to house seeking alms, which would be their livelihood. People revered them for their knowledge and wisdom. The caste system was later changed and became based on the birth of the individual. The erosion of our value system started with wealth being given prominence over knowledge. In today's era, being born in a rich family is considered more respectable than being born in a family of scientists and professors. It is a sad but true reflection of our times that our bank balances and lifestyles determine the respect we command in society.

By looking at terrorist attacks like 9/11 or 26/11, we should try and understand just how efficiently human intelligence, combined with systemic planning, can destroy lives. How were any of the lives that were lost in these attacks responsible? What fault did they commit?

If we do not channelize our lives towards the betterment of human life and uphold a value system, it can lead to a devastating impact. We need to programme our mind to be able to distinguish good from evil and make the right decision. It is important that each of us understands our qualities and is driven towards a path of self-development for the greater good. Just like blood flows through our veins, all of us have goodness deep in our heart. We only need our inner self to realize it through self-awakening. The Dalai Lama could have preached violence when he was forced to leave his homeland in the 1950s. Yet, he chose to believe in non-violence and peace, and preached the same. Our choices make us who we truly are.

Self-improvement for Nirvana

It is important to aim for perfection when we try to imbibe in ourselves a spirit of betterment. Every single time Usain Bolt takes the running track, he tries to beat his previous record. Every single time Michael Phelps competes in a swimming event, he tries to create a new world record. Every top professional in the world of sports, or any other field, is driven by an inner desire to better themselves. Every single day, they strive harder to create better versions of themselves. Their desire for perfection is what motivates them towards their goals. However, we are perfect in our imperfections. Sometimes we need to accept our shortcomings and try to work on those. A boss may need to overlook his subordinates' faults and instead focus on their strengths, which will provide them the necessary confidence to overcome their weaknesses. At other times, we just need to accept ourselves as we are.

While Nirvana is viewed as the attainment of peace, is it possible to attain it without achieving our aspirations? The answer is a clear no. If our mind is driven by success, can it attain peace without achieving that success? Consider, for example, the Indian cricket team captain, Virat Kohli. In each of the matches that he plays, his motivation level and eagerness to succeed are extremely visible on the field. For someone like him, the path to perfection is through excellence in his chosen profession. His way of attaining Nirvana is leading his team to victory through his performance as a player and as captain of the team. Only when his team succeeds is he able to sleep peacefully. Now consider that he wins one match—does he give up on his performance for the next match? No—instead, he practices even harder and keeps improving every single time. Attaining Nirvana and achieving aspirations are parallel paths, and coming closer to Nirvana can also help one attain one's aspirations. A person who achieves his targets without attachment is more likely to be promoted than someone else with emotional baggage. Such a person will be keener on attaining excellence in his activity than receiving appreciation from others. As he pursues his activity with single-minded focus, he is able to achieve his goal. Success is purely a function of excellence in any activity.

Similarly, we too need to keep developing ourselves by distinguishing between right and wrong. We can only succeed if this demarcation is clear in our minds. Leakage of exam papers in medical and engineering exams is extremely common. In fact, there are dedicated rackets for this that involve everyone from ministers and college professors to printing presses and coaching institutes. Are they not destroying the future of this country for a few thousand rupees? Now let us imagine that some of the students who end up paying for these leaked papers top the exam. These students end up becoming doctors and engineers and then build faulty structures or administer wrong medicines to patients. In a bid to succeed without putting in the required effort, they are putting several lives at risk in the future. Is this the kind of success that we should strive for?

Real success lies in our ability to help others. What we should all aspire for is donating to those who are needy and creating a difference in their lives. The Bill and Melinda Gates Foundation is a prime example in this regard. The Foundation contributes 1 billion USD every year to social causes globally. Surely, Bill Gates, the co-founder of Microsoft, could have kept all his wealth to himself. Instead, he decided to make a contribution to society. Such feelings of care and humility should define us as humans. These should not just be our individual goals, but a common desire for the betterment of mankind. Wealth is important, but only upto a point. Beyond that point, wealth has no utility. Once we have enough wealth to meet our needs, we should turn to helping others.

Every action we perform is driven by a motivation

that can be virtuous or non-virtuous, depending on our intentions. We should drive ourselves on the virtuous path in order to motivate ourselves towards enlightenment. It was a relentless quest for truth that drove Prince Siddhartha towards enlightenment, towards becoming Lord Buddha, and we can clearly perceive the change that occurred in him during this phase. He was able to understand the true nature of life, our connections with each other, and our duties as humans. It is this enlightenment that we should try to seek in our lives. This will involve tremendous levels of soul-searching in order to find the path that is best suited for us.

For self-improvement and to move towards Nirvana or enlightenment, we can follow a few simple steps:

- **Follow the right path**: It is important to visualize the possible consequences of an action before committing to it, because each of our actions can unfold in several possible ways, with different consequences.
- **Practise a life of austerity:** Extravagant displays of wealth and success have never helped anyone. They create more enemies than friends. On the other hand, if we practise a culture of austerity and focus on contributing to the community at large, it creates an unmatched spirit of bonhomie and friendship.
- **Meditate**: The power of meditation is well known.

It grants our mind understanding and enables us to focus on our goal. We need to understand the importance of life and good health and be in grateful for all that we possess.

- **Exercise and practise yoga**: It is equally important to regularly exercise to keep our body fit. A healthy body houses a healthy mind and spirit. Exercise, especially the practice of yoga, can boost our inner spirit and provide us strength in the face of adversity. It can also provide us longevity and ensure that our mind is free from negative thoughts.
- **Maintain a healthy diet**: Feeding our mind with positive thoughts is not the only important thing. It is also necessary to ensure that we consume a healthy diet. A balanced diet, coupled with a healthy lifestyle, ensures that our body can physically experience events. Physical experiences are as important as mental ones for success. Our positive thoughts help us in performing good deeds. A person who is hungry will think about food instead of performing a task.
- **Define a goal**: It helps to define your goals for every stage of life. These goals need not be self-centric. They must be inclusive, which implies that apart from your personal ambitions, you need to also focus on the greater good of others around you in the community.
- **Build positive relationships**: Man is a social animal

and needs a network of positive relationships in order to lead a successful life. This is possible only by adopting a culture of compassion and love towards one another.

- **Cultivate a sense of gratitude**: A sense of gratitude helps one to remain humble and thankful for everything one has in life. It helps us to appreciate our possessions and the people in our lives, as well as contribute to our community.
- **Have a mentor**: It is equally important to have a good mentor in our lives who shows us the path ahead when we are struggling. Even religious scriptures can help us to find purpose in our lives. The scriptures help us to differentiate between good and evil and teach us the importance of treading the right path.

We get sweet fruit if we sow the right seed. Similarly, when we harbour positive feelings towards others, it brings about good for those around us and ourselves. The ability to do good for oneself without affecting others adversely eventually makes all the difference. The truth of all enlightenment can be perceived in two halves: one that comprises our actual ability to experience it and another where we are unable to see it directly. It is important to understand the difference. When we talk about the ability to experience, we refer to the state where we are able to sense the change ourselves. For example, a state of emptiness in our mind, without any anger or fear, is similar to that of the Supreme Being—in a constant state of bliss, devoid of pain or suffering. If we keep our mind detached, we, too, will not experience pain. Our mind should try to create a feeling of thoughtlessness and expand it to start experiencing this void within itself. The state of enlightenment that cannot be experienced directly refers to feelings of compassion and love. If we start feeling and thinking well about everyone, it amounts to enlightenment. Only the wisest can claim to have the authority to have good thoughts all the time. By thinking well of others, we enter a phase where our minds are always calm and devoid of any negative feelings. We begin to feel that we are no different from the world around them. We begin to see ourselves as part of every creature around us.

It is important to understand that such self-control within us can only be obtained with years of practice, dedication and patience. Our journey towards self-development and self-discovery will be futile if we lack patience. We will begin the journey whole-heartedly, but then give it up midway if we do not see the results immediately. Our mind is complex; it will not adjust to the changed environment immediately. Just like years of addiction to alcohol do not go away in a single day, our changed way of thinking will also require patience and practice.

Nirvana in Service

Humans, bestowed with knowledge and wisdom, should

engage in the act of giving and helping others. Just as we tend to protect others from suffering, we need to heal our own pain. It is only by guiding others and following a moral path that we can aim to attain Nirvana. We should be mentally strong enough to bear any form of hardship, and should look at pain and suffering as inherent parts of our lives. Just as life and death are inseparable, so are pain and suffering. It is this realization that will help keep our mind strong and guide it towards attaining Nirvana. We must also be patient in our lives and focus on performing our duties instead of following rituals blindly.

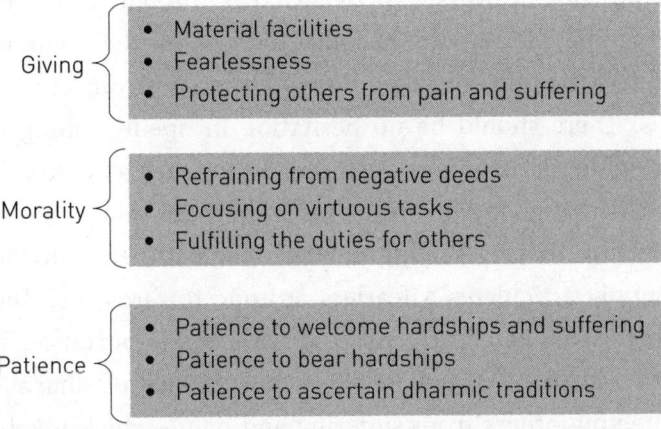

Figure 3: Different aspects of Giving, Morality and Patience

The idea of giving may be broken down into three levels: giving material facilities, encouraging fearlessness, and protecting others from suffering and pain. It is important to understand that there is a right time and situation for giving. For example, it is inappropriate to offer someone food during Ramzan. Our act of giving should not affect anyone adversely—be it their mental health or their self-esteem. Similarly, after helping someone, if we keep telling others about what we did, trying to take credit in order to promote ourselves, there is no purpose in such giving. It becomes merely a scheme to increase one's level of respect in society. Just like actions should be performed without expecting anything in return, so should we perform the act of giving. We must focus only on the act and the positive impact it creates. The second level of giving, encouraging fearlessness, means that through our act of giving, people should become fearless in their conduct and feel the power to stand up against any wrongs in their lives. There should be no hesitation in openly calling out that which is wrong as wrong and the truth as truth. The true idea of giving involves practising these values in order to ensure that by staying on the right path, an individual naturally articulates a fearless attitude towards life. Then, only the righteous path will hold value and importance. The third aspect of giving involves the practice of dharma—protecting others from suffering and pain—which involves helping others understand the transient nature of life and the idea that rather than searching for material happiness, they should seek joy within themselves.

Similarly, the principles of morality as reflected in our deeds are also comprised of three levels: morality of refraining from negative deeds; morality of virtuous acts and morality of fulfilling the activities of others. Unless an individual is virtuous, he cannot help others. The quality of virtue can only be developed if a person is able to distinguish right from wrong. Those unable to identify this path cannot achieve the desired purpose of helping anyone.

Our patience, too, may be divided into three stages: patience to welcome hardships and sufferings; patience to bear those hardships and patience to ascertain dharmic traditions. It is important to note that unless we are inclined towards the dharmic traditions of renunciation and Moksha, we will not be driven by a need to welcome hardships and sufferings. Throughout our life, we will try to avoid or run away from suffering and be driven to only seek the pleasures of life. Our mind will be tricked into thinking that life is all about enjoyment. Often, parents are left in old-age homes while their children pursue their own dreams. Thus we tend to ignore those who have played the most major role in shaping our future. Another clear case in point is young students preferring to indulge in alcohol and drugs in their mistaken understanding of these habits as 'cool'. Many of them feel that life is all about having fun. They do not realize that soon they will wither away, and only their deeds will be left as the legacy of their life. It is important to realize that we are all so intricately connected that our struggles today will have a direct bearing on future generations. If we work hard today, we secure our future, as our deeds will not just impact us but also the generations that follow. It is necessary, therefore, to gain clarity on the kind of legacy one would like to leave behind. There are no gains in life without struggles. Even a small cocoon struggles to break through its chrysalis to become a butterfly. All of us admire the beauty of the butterfly, without realizing the hardships it has undergone to become one. Similarly, in order to awaken spiritually and attain Nirvana, one needs to be patient.

We try to understand events and situations through our analytical mind and experiences. Our struggle to imbibe positive qualities in our minds is real. We often look for shortcuts in order to achieve success and happiness. This leads us to take wrong decisions which may not uphold ethical and moral values. It is important to use our analytical mind to bridge the gap between perceived reality and actual reality. If we constantly practise self-development, we can open the secret doors to keeping ourselves free from all negative thoughts. We can inculcate a spirit of working towards our own betterment, which will drive us towards the attainment of Nirvana.

Food for Thought:

List five areas in your life where you would like to improve yourself. How would you do this? Try to follow these steps for a week and review your progress. Now continue to perform these steps till you achieve the goal of perfection in these five areas.

5
Nirvana Through Equanimity

Never let the future disturb you. You will meet it, if you have to, with the same weapons of reason which today arm you against the present.

—Marcus Aurelius,
philosopher and author of *Meditations*

Equanimity is a state of psychological stability that is undisturbed by any external event. These events, which would normally impact any other person, can include extreme, unforeseen circumstances such as the sudden death of an earning family member or the devastating impact of a hurricane or a flood. Humans, by default, are sensitive beings. We mostly react to situations rather than respond to them. However, our brains work differently when we are actually a part of such extreme, unpredictable situations.

Normally, our brains look for quick fixes to problems in one of two ways. The first way involves carefully analysing the situation and then responding to it. In such situations, we become so perplexed when bogged down by too many random thoughts and ideas that we either procrastinate or fail to act, largely because our mind stays tied up in a multitude of emotions. These emotions can be positive, negative or neutral. In such a state, it is difficult for anyone to react accurately. The second way involves reacting quickly to situations and responding in the moment—for example, quickly jumping into a river to save a drowning person. History, too, is replete with examples that show that humans will never respond effectively unless there is a crisis, as it is then that their survival instinct takes over.

Consider the case of a stock broker during the crash of 2008, when leading companies globally either went bankrupt or lost nearly half of their market capitalization. It was a crisis and the market responded with a huge amount of selling. Everyone followed, and most exited the market. The same market is booming today, and analysts are placing 'buy' calls on some of the same companies investors had lost faith in back in 2008. The problem with human psychology is that our immediate response is always exaggerated, or we tend to overemphasize our reactions when overwhelmed by a sudden loss. Few of us are capable of absorbing the shocks in our life with equanimity. For example, the death of an immediate family member can negatively impact the best of people and create a void in their lives. Now imagine a person who can remain stoic in such situations. Such persons can remain calm even during a crisis, and that stoicism enables them to take the appropriate action for the moment. A person who has had a death in his family will be emotional, and this will impact his mental peace. He will tend to react in a rash manner to situations. On the other hand, a person who is calm in such a situation will retain his composure and accept that death is a natural outcome of life.

Maintaining a state of equanimity has been given importance across various religions. In fact, saints and priests must remain in an undisturbed mental state of equanimity to be able to offer the right advice to disciples. Even athletes need to maintain their composure and equanimity before a key game. In Hinduism, the term for equanimity is derived from the Sanskrit word Samavatam. It means giving up of all forms of attachment to success or failure, and is considered a form of yoga or a path to Nirvana, characterized by a balanced and composed mental state—one of no emotion. The performance of our duties should not be linked to any expectations of a reward.

Equanimity for Peace

It is important to cultivate a sense of detachment from our thoughts. Say, you are angry with Mr Sharma. You will begin to perceive him as an object and start considering him unkind, uncaring or despicable, and blame him entirely for whatever you are upset about. Such judgements about people arise when we are unable to view things from a neutral standpoint. Our judgement of a person is clouded due to our attachment to some other thing. Someone else in our shoes, without such biases, may decide differently.

Another Sanskrit term for equanimity is upeksha (non-attachment), which is actually one of the essentials for having a peaceful mind, along with maitri (love and kindness), karuna (compassion) and mudita (joy). It would be difficult to attain any progress on the path of Nirvana without achieving upeksha or dispassion. A steady and stable mind can also be attained through meditation and pranayama, which create a balance between our mental and physical health. In order to attain this state of equanimity, an individual needs to dedicate himself to mindfulness through regular self-observation. In order to take charge of our mind, we need to, consciously and with full awareness, acknowledge and sift through our various thoughts and desires—to consistently programme our mind to remain on the right path. If we can guide our mind, we can take charge of our emotions and act positively in all situations.

In Buddhism, too, upeksha is considered one of the four sublime attitudes. It is described as being neither a thought nor an emotion, but a steady state of realization of the reality of the world around us. A mind that has equanimity is without any hostility or ill feelings towards others. As such a mind considers all states as equal, it has no reason to consider any event as bad or any human as an enemy. It lacks any desire to harbour negative thoughts that lead to self-destruction through a cycle of desire, greed and grief.

Abrahamic religions such as Judaism, Christianity

and Islam, too, echo equanimity as an imperative for our spiritual progress. In Judaism, equanimity, referred to as *Menuhat ha-Nefesh* or *Yishuv ha-Da'at* is considered a critical foundation for moral and spiritual development. It is considered an important element for the development of an individual's personality and self. In Christianity, too, equanimity is considered essential for an individual to carry out his religious duties towards society. It is important that our mind is calm at all times so that our judgement is not biased. Even the word 'Islam' is derived from the Arabic word *aslama*, which means that peace comes only from total surrender and acceptance. One of the core beliefs of Islam is that every event occurs by the will of God. This belief can only be accepted if one has a mind unaffected by external circumstances.

We can see that equanimity has been described as a key requirement across religions. There is no doubt that only a calm and steady mind can lead a person towards Nirvana. The key question, therefore, is—how may a person achieve and cultivate equanimity? There are some simple steps that an individual can follow in order to achieve a state of equanimity—

1. **Understand your present situation:** It is important to realize our present state. We must understand both our physical and mental state and analyze both the pros and cons. We often tend to demean what we already have in our pursuit of happiness. We ignore our family in the

pursuit of wealth; we ignore our health and consume alcohol. We often long to be different from what we are now. We desire a different life than the one we currently have, and this causes dissatisfaction and longing. When we try to change circumstances not within our control, it causes unnecessary pain and suffering—not only for us, but perhaps for others, too. Equanimity should not be seen as resignation to fate. Instead, it should be seen as the acceptance of one's present situation. A person who is sick may look at other people who are fine and feel sad. Alternatively, he can accept his present situation and start working towards improving his health. Equanimity should not be seen as giving up on circumstances, but rather, accepting our condition and then finding ways to improve it.

2. **Be willing to accept change**: It is extremely vital that we be willing to accept changes in our lives. Just like the world is always changing, so are our lives, like a sequence of consecutive days and nights filled with moments of joy and happiness, grief and sadness. We often tend to perceive permanence in our state of happiness. Instead, we need to accept that it is impermanent and bound to change. Our lives are a sequence of waves, and it is in our best interests that we learn to accept the ephemeral and changing nature of life. If we can learn to accept this as a natural law, we can definitely keep our minds calm. We can tell ourselves in our tough moments that everything around us has a limited period of existence.

In times of grief, we can tell ourselves that this, too, is not permanent. This too shall pass. Human life is not much different from the fates of nation states and civilizations, which are also characterized by their rise and fall.

3. **Take small, baby steps towards equanimity**: It is extremely important that we try to bring about small changes at first in order to realize any significant change in our lives. We need to teach ourselves to remain calm in any situation, regardless of adversity or joy. This is not easy to achieve, as we tend to get carried away in the moment. To achieve a state of equanimity, therefore, first requires an awareness that we are not currently in a state of calm, and then simply practice to achieve that. We also need a lot of patience, without which it is not possible to achieve the same. We need to tell ourselves that good things take time to happen and we must never give up. We must stay calm and keep trying till we succeed.

The significant increase in the rate of crime in our cities stands testimony to the fact that we are facing an emotional crisis and reacting to situations in ways unworthy of humanity. There is an erosion in the collective social values that guide us, as we mostly seek instant gratification. Take, for example, the Christchurch mosque shootings, where people praying in a mosque in New Zealand were shot. When you think about such incidents, you realize that these actions can only be driven by unparalleled rage and hatred, and can never be conceived by a mind that respects human life. The mass shootings that occur all across the United States are further examples of how destructive the human mind has become, attached as it is to the unstable negative emotions of animosity, loathing and hatred. We need to learn to let go of our attachment to such negative emotions.

Letting Go

It is important to understand the principle of letting go. When faced with circumstances beyond our control, we must simply try to stop worrying about them. Our worry actually increases our anxiety, which affects us mentally and unhinges our connection to our value system, driving us to extreme actions. Once we are aware of the negative thoughts running in a loop in our head, we need to detach from them, which can be done by replacing negative thoughts with positive affirmation. For example, when hatred is your key emotion, replace it with an affirmation like 'I am grateful for all the abundance in my life. My heart is open to receiving love.' Repeating an affirmation can replace the loop of a negative thought. When coupled with physical movement, a short bout of exercise, a kickboxing session or simply going for a walk, it has the power to completely replace the negative emotion. This will help in programming our mind to react positively to situations.

We must learn to take life as it comes. Only when we let go of our ego, as reflected in all our emotional states of attachment, desires and expectations, can we achieve momentary peace. If we let go a little more, our moments of peace multiply, and when we let go completely—without experiencing emotions and remaining in a state of equanimity, detached from our physical, mental or emotional circumstances—when we can give it all up—we are able to achieve permanent bliss.

An individual who has achieved equanimity will display certain personality characteristics. These characteristics are reflective of his mind, which will remain balanced under any circumstance. A person with equanimity has knowledge of the transient nature of life and shows a loving attitude towards all living beings. While some attachment is important in our relationships, as we are worldly people, he knows that excessive attachment is always destructive. He has also cultivated a balanced attitude towards all objects—wealth, materialistic possessions and property. He lives an austere life without any personal ambitions of acquiring wealth or material possessions. Such an individual is never blinded by the glitter of this world; nor does he feel the need to pursue any of the varied forms of material wealth. He seeks out associations with the right people with positive attitudes and balanced minds, who provide the motivation to cultivate a similar view of life. Naturally, he instinctively avoids exposure to toxic people, who provide the actual test of his equanimity. Such people are consumed by worldly vices and driven by selfish needs. It is difficult to maintain a state of calm when under the influence of toxic persons with no desire for the betterment of humanity. It is best to avoid such people, who will influence us to tread on the wrong path.

In order to be able to achieve equanimity, we must seek to cultivate mental qualities that naturally support our thought processes when we are faced with critical choices.

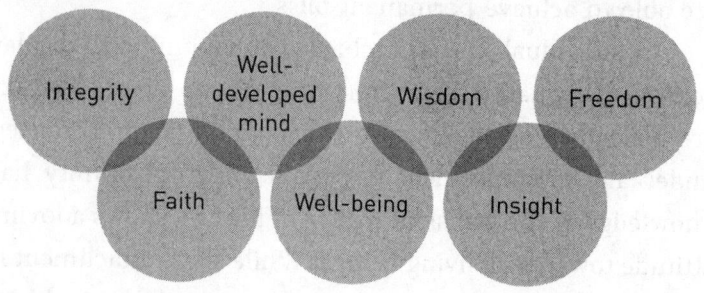

Figure 4: Mental qualities required in order to achieve equanimity

While integrity helps to root our actions in basic honesty and keeps us reliable and upright, a well-developed mind is trained to instinctively discriminate between right and wrong outcomes and helps to keep us on the right path. Wisdom, gained through experience, ensures that we have true freedom to choose, and our decisions are not driven or coloured by worldly attachments. Faith is important in moments of crisis, as it keeps us rooted enough to perform our duties with equanimity, in the firm belief that this too shall pass. Well-being comes from a state of health and happiness—when we eat healthy, exercise and promote positive thoughts. Reflecting on our own experiences as well as others' actions in various situations, or even on the books we read provides valuable insights that help our decision-making process.

It is important to have a balanced outlook towards life if we aim to achieve Nirvana. If our mind is disturbed, we cannot achieve peace. Building an attitude of equanimity provides us with an ability to look through people and situations without bias. This attitude keeps us kind and calm, without any fear, and we are able to attain bliss or Nirvana through our actions. Or, at least, certainly progress towards this state.

Food for thought:

Often people will try to provoke you to get a reaction. One must try to respond and not react to such situations, and if they appear insignificant, it is better to ignore them. What happens to us is not important; it is how we deal with it that determines who we truly are.

6
Nirvana Through Four Noble Truths

The Four Noble Truths are pragmatic rather than dogmatic. They suggest a course of action to be followed rather than a set of dogmas to be believed. The four truths are prescriptions for behaviour rather than descriptions of reality. The Buddha compares himself to a doctor who offers a course of therapeutic treatment to heal one's ills.

—Stephen Bachelor, author

The four noble truths are an integral part of Buddhism. In many ways, they reflect the true nature of human life. 'I teach suffering, its origin, cessation and path. That's all I teach,' declared the Buddha 2,500 years ago. The fundamental nature of Nirvana stems from these four noble truths.

These four truths helped Lord Buddha attain enlightenment during his meditation under the Bodhi tree.

Together, they form the core values of his teachings and can be considered the basic foundation of Buddhism and the path to Nirvana. While I do think that the spirit of Nirvana lies solely in Buddhist culture and faith, these four truths can be applied across religions and are not restricted to followers of just one particular faith.

While we know that the source of our suffering lies in our desires, we are mostly powerless against their force. In fact, our very presence in the mortal world creates desires within us, which in turn makes us long for things which are impermanent in nature. This causes suffering. Nirvana is the path that drives us towards conquering this suffering and understanding the true value of life. If we fail to understand this truth, then, in many ways, despite our successes, our lives will lack value. These four noble truths are:

1. The truth of suffering (Dukkha)
2. The truth of the origin of suffering (Samudāya)
3. The truth of the cessation of suffering (Nirodha)
4. The truth of the path to the cessation of suffering (Magga)

Lord Buddha may be considered a doctor who is trying to find a cure for all suffering in human life. In the first noble truth, he diagnoses the problem. In the second noble truth, he identifies the cause. The third noble truth provides us with the realization that there is a possible cure for our sufferings. The fourth noble truth is where he teaches us the Eightfold Path to achieve this cure. His mode of analysing the cause and effect relationship is reminiscent of the analytical mind that is required to achieve Nirvana. It is this analytical mind that helps us understand the true nature of life and distinguish right from wrong. In some ways, the eight-fold path can be considered as a prescription for the betterment of life.

The First Noble Truth: Suffering (Dukkha)

Suffering can be in many forms. Lord Buddha saw, on his first journey outside his palace, the three forms of human suffering—sickness, old age and death. These three forms taught him about the impermanent nature of human life. Yet our suffering runs much deeper than that. Suffering makes us believe that not only are our lives not ideal, but that they also fail to live up to our expectations. That is when we tend to feel sad, and hence, suffer. Our desires and dreams create restless minds. When we achieve these dreams, we become satisfied; however, this satisfaction is only temporary. After a certain period of time, we again tend to become restless and continue to suffer. Even when we do not have any outward causes like illness or bereavement, we still continue to feel low and disappointed. This is the true nature of human life. Even though it may sound pessimistic that life is full of sorrows and pain, it is the real nature of life. Our path to achieving Nirvana cannot be determined without understanding this basic nature of human life. The good part, though, is that Lord Buddha's teachings also show the path to ending our suffering and pain.

The Second Noble Truth: Origin of Suffering (Samudāya)

In our daily lives, then, we usually suffer pain from a few causes such as thirst, hunger, loss of a loved one, ill health and trust issues with close associates. In fact, trouble in our relationships can be a great cause for pain and suffering. However, there is one cause which is common to all of these; Buddha helped us to identify that cause as desire.

It is our desire that makes us act differently from others. It makes us think only about our own self and our own benefits, rather than considering the society at large. It creates a wall between us and them, as we no longer tend to see ourselves as belonging to a common universe shared by all creation.

According to Buddhism, desire or *tanha* (in Pali) comes in three forms. These are also referred to as the three poisons or three roots of evil, as they can corrupt the human mind. They are regarded as the ultimate causes of pain and suffering.

- Greed and desire, represented in art by a rooster
- Ignorance or delusion, represented by a pig
- Hatred and destructive urges, represented by a snake

The word *tanha* in Pali specifically means craving or misplaced desire. Buddhists also recognize that there can be positive desires, such as the desire for enlightenment and good wishes for others. Such desires need to be cultivated if one wishes to attain Nirvana. Such positive desires help us visualize ourselves in harmony with the other creations around us.

The Third Noble Truth: Cessation of Suffering (Nirodha)

Lord Buddha taught that the way to conquer or extinguish desire, which causes suffering, is to free ourselves from any form of attachment. This creates the possibility of our liberation and of attaining Moksha. While some may argue that such a state is only possible after death, Lord Buddha is an example that it is possible even in a living body. By leading a life without desires, Lord Buddha was able to remove all of his suffering.

We may remove the suffering of a living body through our ability to correctly sense and interpret the conditions causing the suffering. Our mind should adopt a rational approach and not an emotional one. We should try to respond and not react to situations. It is by creating a sense of detachment and disenchantment that one can achieve the same.

If one is to achieve Nirvana, one has to extinguish the three fires of greed, delusion and hatred. This is essential to achieving enlightenment. Without extinguishing these, there is no possible way an individual can attain peace. One might think that once you have achieved Nirvana, you will transcend into a heavenly abode. However, this is not true. On attaining Nirvana, we tend to understand and feel a sense of profound joy without any negative emotions and fears. It can be looked upon as a state of the human mind and should not be considered as a liberation of the human soul. While Hinduism speaks of a cycle of rebirth and eventual attainment of Moksha, Buddhism does not dwell on what happens after one's death. Several other religions are also silent on this matter and disagree with respect to rebirth. Therefore, our focus should be on attaining this mental state in our present by building positive energy around us.

Rather than focusing our energy and thoughts on what happens after this life, we should instead be focused on achieving Nirvana in our present life. We should centre our mind towards removing negative thoughts and focusing on the task in hand. If we question too much, it will be similar to asking too many questions of a doctor who is simply trying to provide medication to cure our illness. Better to focus on getting well, first.

The Fourth Noble Truth: Path to the Cessation of Suffering (Magga)

The final and fourth noble truth is the prescription by Buddha to end all human suffering. Just like a doctor prescribes medicines, the fourth noble truth looks at how we can reach a balanced state in sync with nature. This brings us to the Eightfold Path, which can be seen as a guide to achieving this. This is considered one of the core beliefs in Buddhism and can be applied across religions.

The Eightfold Path is also referred as the middle way or the middle path. Neither does it tell us to lead an extremely austere life nor does it suggest leading a life full of indulgence and pleasure. Instead, it prescribes a balanced life. Lord Buddha felt that leading a balanced life is perhaps the best way to achieve eternal bliss. The Eightfold Path can be visualized as spokes in a wheel, which help balance each other just like our emotions need to be balanced. The eight emotions are not to be taken in any particular order, but should be seen as supporting and reinforcing each other.

The Eightfold Path is given below:

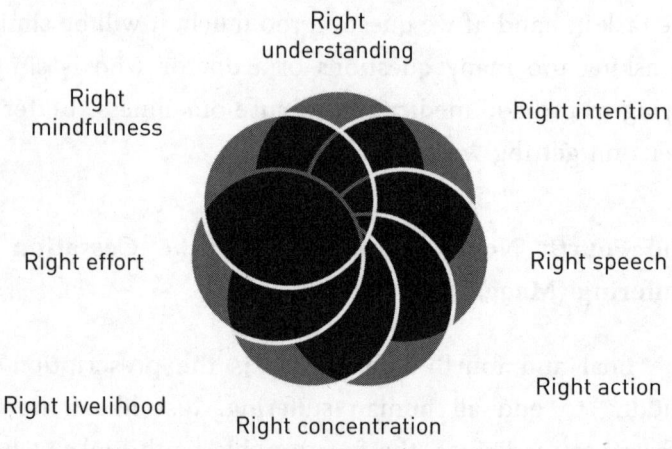

Figure 5: The Eightfold Path

1. **Right understanding—Sammā ditthi**
   Accept the teachings of Lord Buddha. However, do not follow the teachings blindly. Instead, analyse; and only when you are convinced, follow the teachings. We should use our own analysis to determine the validity of the teachings. This will help to build our faith and re-affirm our self-belief.
2. **Right intention—Sammā sankappa**
   It is equally important to cultivate the right attitude, which should be an outcome of our quest for knowledge and wisdom. We should consider all creations as equal and treat them with respect.
3. **Right speech—Sammā vācā**
   It is important to always speak the truth, even if it creates temporary loss. One should also avoid any form of slander, gossip or abusive talk. In addition, one should avoid speech which can hurt anybody emotionally.
4. **Right action—Sammā kammanta**
   One should understand the difference between right and wrong and always stay on the path of performing the right action. It is important to behave peacefully and harmoniously and avoid actions such as stealing, killing or over-indulgence in sensual pleasures.
5. **Right livelihood—Sammā ājīva**
   We must avoid causing harm to another lifeform for our own benefit. We should not exploit others or kill animals in order to earn our livelihood. We should also avoid intoxicants and weapons.

6. **Right effort—Sammā vāyāma**
   It is important to always have a positive state of mind. Whenever one feels any negative emotions, one should free himself from them and try to cultivate positive emotions. In addition, one should prevent negative emotions from arising in future by following the Eightfold Path.
7. **Right mindfulness—Sammā sati**
   One should develop awareness of the body, sensations and state of mind. When we understand a situation and our state of mind, we can respond appropriately.
8. **Right concentration—Sammā samādhi**
   We should stay focused on our goal, which will help to prevent negative thoughts.

The eight stages can be grouped into wisdom (right understanding and intention), ethical conduct (right speech, action and livelihood) and meditation (right effort, mindfulness and concentration). The Buddha described the Eightfold Path as a means to enlightenment, like a raft for crossing a river. Once one has reached the opposite shore, one no longer needs the raft and can leave it behind. This is so because, by that time, such values are already deeply ingrained in us. Thus, by following the Eightfold Path and understanding the four noble truths, one can achieve the state of Nirvana.

Food for thought:

The four noble truths describe the cause of suffering and how to attain liberation from it. Now list five things that create positive emotions in you. Try to understand the difference, and condition your mind through regular meditation.

Acknowledgements

This book would not have been possible without the blessings of my late mother, Dr Lina Bhattacharya. She has been instrumental in guiding me, and whatever I achieve in life I owe to her. My wife Arpita was extremely supportive and understanding, without which I do not feel writing this book would have been possible. I would like to thank my father Vishwa Nath Bhattacharya, my elder brother Abhishek and my sister-in-law Pamela, who have constantly supported me through every phase of my life.

I would like to express my gratitude for my publisher Rupa Publications, the editorial team, and my commissioning editor Yamini Chowdhury, for giving me the opportunity to write this book.